D0114489

For Andrea & Claudia

- I F

For Mum & Dad, who helped

- J T

LITTLE TIGER PRESS
1 The Coda Centre, 189 Munster Road, London SW6 6AW
www.littletiger.co.uk
First published in Great Britain 1999
This edition published 2013
Text copyright © Isobel Finn 1999
Illustrations copyright © Jack Tickle 1999
Visit Jack Tickle at www.ChapmanandWarnes.com
Isobel Finn and Jack Tickle have asserted their rights
to be identified as the author and illustrator of this work
under the Copyright, Designs and Patents Act, 1988
Printed in China • LTP/1800/1355/0915
2 4 6 8 10 9 7 5 3

The Very Lazy Ladybird

Isobel Finn

Jack Tickle

LITTLE TIGER PRESS
London

This is the story of
a very lazy ladybird.

She liked to sleep all day . . .

. . . and all night.

Because she slept
all day, and all night,
this lazy ladybird didn't
know how to fly.

One day, the lazy
ladybird wanted to
sleep somewhere else.
But what could she
do if she couldn't fly?

Then the lazy
ladybird had a
very good idea.

When a kangaroo bounded by . . .

...she hopped into her pouch.

But the
kangaroo
liked to
JUMP!

"I can't sleep in here,"
cried the lazy ladybird.
"It's too bumpy."

So when a tiger padded by...

...she hopped onto his back.

But the tiger liked to

ROAR!

"I can't sleep here,"
said the lazy ladybird.
"It's too noisy."

So when a crocodile swam by . . .

...she hopped onto his tail.

But the crocodile liked to

SWISH

his tail in the water.

"I can't sleep here,"
said the lazy ladybird.
"I'll fall into the river!"

So when a monkey swung by . . .

...she hopped onto her head.

But the monkey liked to

SWING

from branch to branch.

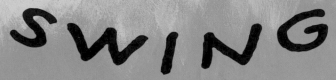

"I can't sleep here," said the lazy ladybird. "I'm feeling dizzy."

So when a bear ambled by . . .

...she hopped onto his ear.

But the bear
liked to

SCRATCH!

"I can't sleep here,"
said the lazy ladybird.
"He'll never sit still."

So when a tortoise plodded by . . .

...she hopped onto her shell.

But the
tortoise liked to

S N O O Z E

in the sun.
"I can't sleep here,"
said the lazy ladybird.
"It's too hot."

So when an elephant walked by . . .

...she hopped onto his trunk.

At last! thought
the lazy ladybird.
I've found someone
who doesn't . . .

jump?

But at that very moment . . .

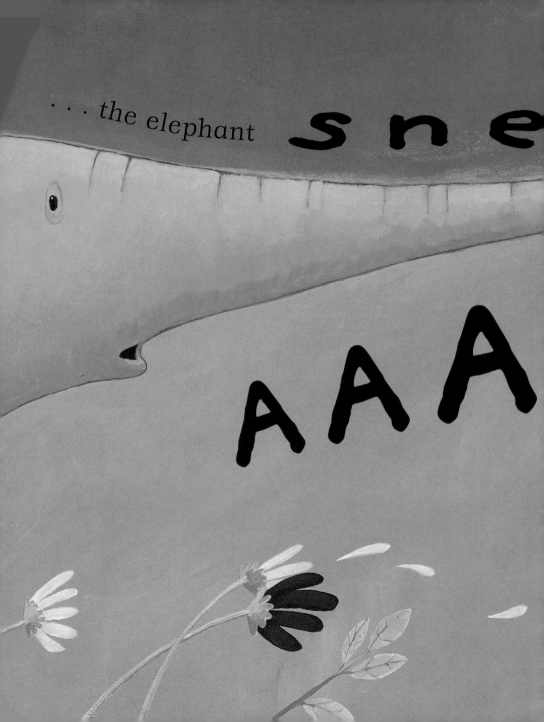

... the elephant **s n e**

AAA

ezed!

CHOOo

And the lazy ladybird . . .

...had to fly at last!

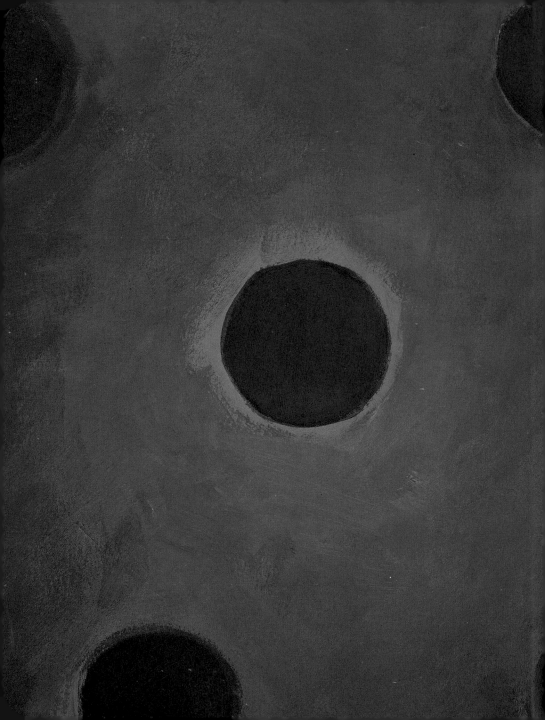